Strawberry Shortcake

20 POM-POM stickers

Strawberry Shortcake's Snow Day

By Megan E. Bryant
Illustrated by Josie Yee

Grosset & Dunlap • New York

Strawberry Shortcake™ © 2003 Those Characters From Cleveland, Inc. Used under license by Penguin Group (USA) Inc.
All rights reserved. Published by Grosset & Dunlap, a division of Penguin Young Readers Group,
345 Hudson Street, New York, NY 10014. GROSSET & DUNLAP is a trademark of
Penguin Group (USA) Inc. Published simultaneously in Canada. Printed in China.

ISBN 0-448-43206-4   C D E F G H I J

One winter morning, Strawberry Shortcake
woke up to a berry big surprise—
Strawberryland was covered in snow!
"It's a snow day—no school!" Strawberry cheered.

Use pom-poms to decorate
Strawberry's and
Custard's night caps.

"Come on, Apple Dumplin'," Strawberry said to her little sister.
"Let's get dressed. We're going to play in the snow!"

Colorful pom-poms
make winter hats and
earmuffs extra nice.

Just then, there was a knock at the door.
"I wonder who that is," Strawberry said.
She opened the door and got another surprise—it was Angel Cake,
Orange Blossom, Ginger Snap, and Huckleberry Pie!
"Hi, Strawberry!" said Huck. "Do you want to come play with us?"
"Of course, I do!" Strawberry said with a big smile.

Decorate their hats, jackets,
and boots with pom-poms.

"I want to go ice skating!" said Angel Cake.
"Peppermint Pond is frozen solid."

"I want to go sledding!" said Orange Blossom.
"There's a big hill behind my orchard!"

"I want to build a snowman!" said Ginger Snap.
"There's lots of fresh snow in Cookie Corners."

"And I want to have a snowball fight!" said Huckleberry Pie.
"I make the biggest snowballs around!"

Make shimmery snowballs
using pom-pom stickers.

"We can do all those fun things—if we take turns!"
Strawberry Shortcake said. Her friends agreed.
So first, they went ice skating.
"Whoops!" said Ginger Snap as she tumbled onto the ice.
"Be careful!" Strawberry said. "It's berry slippery out here!"

Next the friends went sledding.
Everyone trudged through the snow
to the hill behind Orange Blossom Acres.
"Sledding is much more fun when we go down
the hill together!" Strawberry said happily.

After sledding for a long time, Strawberry Shortcake and her friends decided to build snowmen in Cookie Corners. Soon they had made a whole family of snowmen!

Thwack! Somebody threw a snowball at Ginger Snap. It was Huck!
"Look out, Huck!" Ginger called playfully as she
scooped up some snow and shaped it into a big snowball.
Soon everyone was throwing snowballs at each other!

Decorate with your pom-pom stickers.

Next they went back to Strawberry's house for some yummy hot chocolate.
"Mmm, Strawberry, you make the best hot chocolate!" Orange Blossom
said as the kids warmed up in Strawberry's cheery cottage.
"Thank you berry much!" Strawberry replied. "I love hot chocolate!"

When it was time for everyone to go home,
Strawberry walked her friends to the door.
"Oh my goodness!" said Ginger Snap. "It's snowing again!"
"That's great!" Strawberry exclaimed. "We can play in the snow
again tomorrow! Good night, everybody. See you in the morning!"

Use pom-pom stickers as soft, fluffy snowflakes.

Enjoy these berry fun winter crafts—including one that uses sparkly pom-pom stickers!

MARSHMALLOW SNOWMEN

For each snowman, you will need:
3 large marshmallows
toothpicks
red thin licorice rope
black thin licorice rope

1. Stick the toothpicks into each end of one marshmallow. This marshmallow will be the snowman's middle.
2. Stick the other two marshmallows on the top and bottom.
3. Use small pieces of the black licorice to make eyes, a nose, and a mouth (stick them on with a toothpick).
4. Use a three-inch section of the red licorice to tie around the snowman's neck and make a scarf!

PRETTY PAPER SNOWFLAKES

You will need:
typing or construction paper
scissors
glitter
pom-poms

1. Fold a sheet of paper in half.
2. Cut out a half-circle along the crease. Then fold it in half.
4. Cut out shapes and designs on all edges.
3. Unfold it and decorate it with glitter and pom-pom stickers.

YUMMY HOT CHOCOLATE

Make sure there is a grown-up in the kitchen to help you make this yummy hot chocolate!

You will need:
2 tablespoons cream
2 tablespoons cocoa powder
2 tablespoons sugar
2 cups milk
whipped cream, marshmallows,
chocolate shavings (optional)

1. In a small pot over low heat, mix the cream, cocoa powder, and sugar until they form a thick paste.
2. Slowly pour in the milk. Stir constantly until all ingredients are combined and the milk is very warm.
3. Carefully pour the hot chocolate into two cups.
4. Add whipped cream, marshmallows, or chocolate shavings to make it extra yummy! Makes 2 servings—one for you and one for a berry good friend!